FOR A HORSE NAMED CORWIN

FOR A HORSE NAMED CORWIN

A SCI-FI/WESTERN STORY

ROBERT J. MCCARTER

LITTLE HUMMINGBIRD PUBLISHING

Cover image © istockphoto.com/portfolio/vikarus

ISBN: 978-1-941153-19-2

Visit Robert's website at: RobertJMcCarter.com

Published by:

Little Hummingbird Publishing

P.O. Box 23518

Flagstaff, AZ 86002

www.LittleHummingbird.com

Little Hummingbird Publishing is a division of Arapas, Inc. Find more about Arapas at: www.Arapas.com.

For Meg and Nelly...
Thanks for taking me back to the past.

This story was originally published in 2018 as part of *Anomalous Readings: Thirteen Curious and Confounding Tales* and appears there with 12 of my other stories.

FOR A HORSE NAMED CORWIN

EVAN WILCOX REIGNED IN HIS HORSE AND STOOD UP IN THE stirrups. The desert of planet Valdrin stretched before him in all directions, seeming to be an endless expanse of sage brush, sand, and prickly pear cactus. He felt a tingle go up and down his spine. Something wasn't right.

"Bad," his mount, Corwin, said, shaking his head and rattling his tack.

Wilcox nodded and then remembering the horse couldn't see the gesture, added, "You got that right, brother." Wilcox sniffed the air and smelled nothing but sweat, horse, and dust. He scanned the horizon but saw nothing but the distant mountains and heat rising off the land. He closed his eyes and listened carefully and heard-- nothing. Not the slithering of a snake as it moved from one rock to another; not the scamper of a jackrabbit, scared into motion by the snake's approach; not the sigh of a coyote as it slept through the hottest part of the day. Nothing.

Wilcox adjusted his wide brimmed hat, eased back into the saddle, and brushed his thumb against the back of his left ear. There a nerve bundle triggered the release of a hormone that made his cochlea more sensitive, enhancing his sense of hearing. Wilcox, while purely biological, was no longer purely human.

Still he heard nothing but the rattle of the brush in the slight breeze and the breathing of his mount.

Wilcox swallowed hard; he had a sour taste in his mouth, like a rotten lemon. The taste of fear. "Git, Corwin," he said with a grimace, urging the horse from a standstill to a gallop. Wilcox didn't know what was wrong, but he knew something was. The animals knew it, none of them moving a muscle. And Corwin knew it too; he cooperated with unusual vigor. Wilcox rose up in the saddle as the animal galloped beneath him.

When he was a hundred meters out, Wilcox turned and looked back; the spot he and Corwin had just been occupying was shimmering. Not with the heat of the desert but with the hum of the Ancestors.

It had been more than a generation since the Ancestors had visited, long enough so that the young began to doubt their existence, and the old had stopped telling the stories about how they survived. Long enough for vigilance to end.

But Wilcox knew better. He had long dreaded their return. Valdrin is a preserve, formed in the mold of a long dead society from humanity's past, and intent on keeping humanity pure. A place where a strict level of technology is enforced and altered biologicals, like Corwin and Wilcox, are not welcome.

The shimmering resolved into a tight spherical shape with a fuzzy splotch of color in the center starting to come into focus... starting to look like men on their horses. Above the sound of Corwin's hooves striking the ground Wilcox could hear a high-pitched hum that hurt his ears. He thumbed the back of his left ear again, returning his hearing to normal.

"Real. Bad," Corwin gasped as his pace quickened.

Wilcox turned away from the scene of the arriving Ancestors and leaned close to Corwin's neck. "You said it," he said. "Run, my friend, run!"

WILCOX COULD FEEL CORWIN'S FATIGUE, THE HORSE'S BREATH ragged, sweat coating his body. The horse had run long and hard as the flat desert had turned into rolling hills, but Salkin City was still a good ways off. "Ease up, boy," Wilcox told him and the horse slowed to a walk.

He looked behind and didn't see anything. He hoped that they hadn't seen him. He didn't want the Ancestors to ever see them. They wouldn't look kindly on him or Corwin.

Wilcox's plan was simple. Make it to Salkin City before the Ancestors, pick up supplies, head for the mountains, and don't look back.

But, even Corwin couldn't run forever. Wilcox saw a thin tendril of smoke in the distance and let out a sigh of relief. Maybe, just maybe, he could get what he needed there and not have to go to Salkin City. He reigned in Corwin, dismounted, and wrapped the reigns around the saddle horn. He wobbled briefly, his legs weak from the long gallop, before walking towards the smoke.

"Thirsty," Corwin said as he followed.

"I'm working on it, buddy."

"MA'AM," WILCOX SAID HOLDING UP HIS HANDS, FEELING A trickle of sweat slide down his back, "there is no need for that."

The woman brought the shotgun to her shoulder and said, "Well I think there is. Now get off my property."

Wilcox studied her. She wore pants and a shirt made of coarse cloth and had her long black hair braided in the back. Her hands were rough and her face was dirty. Even so, Wilcox caught a whiff of soap among the sweat. All in all, he reckoned she knew how to use that shotgun. He backed up a step, his right hand going to

Corwin's neck. "It's my horse, Ma'am. He's ridden long and hard and needs a drink, if you would be so kind."

She lowered the shotgun and studied the horse, her eyes quickly appraising Corwin's condition.

"What kind of a man rides his horse that hard?" she asked.

"A desperate man," Wilcox said lowering his eyes. "I have news that might make your hospitality worthwhile."

"What news?" she asked raising her shotgun again.

"I'm sorry, Ma'am, but can you tell me your name? I haven't been in these parts for a while, and I'm afraid I don't recognize you. And, it just seems impolite to have a conversation with someone I haven't been introduced to. My name is Wilcox, and this is Corwin."

"I'm Sadie Larkin," the woman said with a sharp nod. "Now say your piece."

Wilcox nodded. "The information I have is valuable. And after I tell it to you, I hope you will consider not only watering Corwin, but giving me whatever food you might that is travel worthy. I--"

"Spit it out, Mr. Wilcox," Sadie said, cocking the shotgun.

"Yes, Ma'am," Wilcox said with a tip of his hat. "The Ancestors have returned."

Wilcox watched as her jaw opened and she blinked rapidly. He followed her eyes to a relatively fresh grave and met her gaze when it returned to him.

"You lie," she said.

"I do not, Ma'am." Wilcox said.

"Ancestors," Corwin said the pronunciation a bit garbled. While Corwin's tongue and vocal cords were more suited to speech than a standard horse, it wasn't as flexible as a person's. "Thirsty. Please."

Sadie lowered the shotgun and held it limp in her grasp. She nodded from Corwin towards the watering trough, her gaze returning again to the grave. "The Ancestors are here?" she mumbled.

"Yes Ma'am," Wilcox said, "and they'll be about the Purge. If you have anything to hide, like Corwin and I do, I suggest you pack up and go."

"SORRY, BOY," WILCOX SAID AS HE RUBBED THE HORSE DOWN, apologizing for the long gallop. He had removed the saddle and blanket and was rubbing the horse's white flank with fresh straw Sadie Larkin had provided. He loved the scent of horses, all clean sweat and power. People often smelled bad when they sweat but horses didn't. It was a purer, cleaner thing, free of the tangle of the darker human emotions.

"Ancestors," Corwin replied.

Wilcox sighed. He feared there was no escaping them. That the decisions of his youth to go off planet and alter himself were finally going to catch up to him. That they had too far to go, and even Corwin did not have the stamina to take them there.

"He's so big, so beautiful," Sadie said as she led another, smaller horse towards Corwin and Wilcox.

"That he is, Mrs. Larkin," Wilcox agreed. "What's the mare for?"

"She's for you."

"I don't understand, Ma'am."

"You are going to ride her to town. You are going to warn those in Salkin City of the coming of the Ancestors."

Wilcox just stared at her, his mouth open.

"You need supplies," she continued. "I have them. Corwin needs rest. You warn the city, and I'll have the cart packed by the time you return. We can leave then."

He studied her face. It was earnest and serious, not a trace or hint of humor. She had washed it while she was inside, and he saw that she was more than a little pretty, with a sprinkling of freckles perched on her high cheek bones. She had eyes that seemed to reflect the blue of the sky and full lips. He had been calling her Ma'am, as was respectful, but he finally saw her as a woman.

"Sorry," he said, turning back to his horse. He pulled a curry comb out of his saddlebag and began brushing Corwin. He noticed that the horse was watching the exchange carefully.

As the seconds slowly passed, he expected her to argue with him. To tell him it was the right thing to do, that everyone should have a chance to avoid the Purge and the judgment of the Ancestors. He stood there pretending to be totally absorbed in what he was doing, pretending he didn't know warning Salkin City was the right thing to do.

The minutes ticked by. He brushed; she stood there with the mare. He wasn't used to this. In his experience women made a big fuss when men didn't do what they ought. The silence weighed on him until he couldn't stand it anymore.

"Corwin..." he began.

"Go," the horse said. "Help."

Wilcox nodded and took the reins of the mare from Sadie. He expected to see a smile on her face, but instead he saw a look of grim resignation, a look that seemed at home on her face.

"You best be ready when I come back," he grunted as he mounted the mare. "We'll be out of time and need to head towards the mountains." He pointed southwest towards a tall snow covered peak.

"I'll be ready," she said and he believed it.

———

Wilcox knew how to ride a horse. He had been riding before he was walking. But this mare was not Corwin. She would not turn at the slightest pressure of his knee, or heed his verbal commands. It took him a few miles to get the feel of riding a normal horse. A natural horse.

And that was it. Natural. The Ancestors would judge this

horse as natural and Corwin as unnatural. They would judge Wilcox with his enhanced senses and his improved nervous system as unnatural. And he and Corwin, they would...

What would they do to them? It had been more than a generation since they came and the tales the grandfathers told grew each year in the telling. If the oldest were to be believed, those that have lived through several visits from the Ancestors, then Wilcox and Corwin would be tortured and killed.

On this planet only that which is natural is allowed. Only limited technology is tolerated. All else is punishable.

Wilcox spurred the mare into a gallop as he headed for Salkin City.

THE HITCH UP SALOON WAS CROWED FOR MID-DAY. IT WASN'T just the desperate and lonely, the saloon was so full that Wilcox had to push his way through the crowd as he made his way towards bar.

"What's going on?" he asked Martin Aster, who had a mug of beer in his hand. Aster was the undertaker and didn't frequent the saloon during the day.

"It's Taylor, he struck a rich vein of iridium. He's been buying drinks for hours." The plump man's speech was slurred as he raised his mug into the air, sloshing beer on the stained wooden floor.

Wilcox nodded and continued plowing towards the bar, his nose wrinkled against the smell of sour beer, urine, and too many bodies. Maybe this was his lucky day, so many citizens of Salkin City in one place. As he approached the bar he spotted the muscular form of Herbert Taylor. Taylor caught his eye as he approached and said, "Wilcox, my friend. Have a drink." He nodded to Hunter, the old wisp of a man that was tending bar, who poured Wilcox a whisky.

"Now you are not the only Salkin native," Taylor continued, "to hit it big. To me!" he cried.

A chorus of "To Taylor!" echoed around the big man as everyone drank. Wilcox shot back his own whiskey, letting it burn its way down his throat, and then without saying a word climbed up onto the bar.

"Excuse me, might I have your attention," he shouted. But the men kept drinking, the saloon girls kept flirting, and the piano man kept playing. Wilcox knew he didn't have much time, that none of them had much time. He pulled his gun out and shot into the floor. He knew what the upstairs of the saloon was used for, so he shot down for fear of his bullet hitting someone up there.

The piano came to a jangling stop as the noise in the saloon decreased, and all eyes found their way to Wilcox. He saw a few hands go to their guns, and Wilcox quickly holstered his. He wasn't here for a fight. "Sorry, folks, I have an announcement, and I'll keep it quick."

The saloon grew quiet, a chorus of annoyed faces looking at Wilcox.

"The Ancestors are coming," he said.

The saloon erupted in noise but a different kind of noise. There were shouts of fear, cries of doubt, and the scuffling of boots as some of the patrons left. Wilcox stood there and let the sound wash around him until one shout rose above the rest.

"Liar, you're a liar, Evan Wilcox," Taylor yelled.

"I am not lying, Taylor," Wilcox replied. "I was far to the east on the flat desert. I had been scouting around Diablo Canyon, heard told there might be some iridium deposits there. On my way back, the desert got dead quiet and I saw the sphere. I saw the bodies materializing in it. It was the Ancestors, no doubt."

"Liar," Taylor repeated. "The Ancestors are just a story our folks used to scare us. They ain't real."

"Then why don't we have electricity?" Wilcox asked. "Why don't we have flying ships or land machines or engines that run on anything but steam? Why are we so backwards when the rest of the worlds are so advanced? I've been there Taylor. I've seen these wonders. It's the Ancestors that enforce our low level of technology, keep us scratching in the dirt."

Taylor snorted and took a drink of his beer. "Truth told, we are a low technology world. It is the basis on which we were founded, the charter on which this planet was settled. That's it and nothing more. We don't need no boogey man to enforce this. We do it by choice."

"You always were dumb, Taylor, weren't you?" Wilcox said. He raised his voice and spoke to the crowd. "Listen to Taylor if you all want. But I am telling the truth. The Ancestors are coming and if you've got tech to hide, you best go hide it and hide yourself. For my part, I'll be headed out of here now."

"Truth is, Wilcox, some of us like it the way it is," Taylor growled. "Some of us will keep our riches here on this planet, will use it to make this a better place, and not run off to see what kind of sick depravities humankind has come to. Some of us won't change what we are no matter how much money we have." The big man paused, taking out a handkerchief and wiping his sweating brow. "Ah hell, forget Wilcox. I'm buying!"

The chorus of agreement was deafening. With a shrug Wilcox got off the bar. Let them think what they think. Wilcox sighed, Taylor had told the truth about him--he had left Valdrin, he had immersed himself in the other world's high tech societies, he had changed himself. He elbowed his way through the crowd until he was outside the saloon standing in the bright sunshine.

"Is it true?" a voice said lightly.

Wilcox turned and saw Jimmy Oster. He was the apprentice barber but had a side business in black market goods. Small things like flashlights and GPS units. Things that ran on electricity. Things made off-world. Things that were forbidden. "Yeah, Jimmy, it's true." Wilcox moved to the mare and unwound her reins from the hitching post.

"But... but..." Jimmy stuttered. "Aren't they just legends? Stories our parents tell to scare us, keep us away from tech? I mean, why would a man choose to sleep the centuries way just to... to..."

Wilcox looked him up and down. Jimmy was just twenty. He hadn't been born when the Ancestors were here last. "They're real, Jimmy, and they're coming. When I was six I saw them take our neighbor away." Wilcox's eyes unfocused and his face went blank. "They looked like gods in their glittering armor, sitting tall on their horses." His eyes snapped back into focus as he looked back at Jimmy. "And I just saw them rise up out of the desert." Wilcox pointed east. "They're coming, I swear it. Spread the word."

Jimmy nodded and took a stride down the dirt street before Wilcox stopped him when he said, "And tell the mayor and the sheriff if you come across them."

"Didn't you seem him?" Jimmy asked, "Mayor Bailey is in there. He's drinking Taylor's whisky and laughing at you."

Wilcox kicked the hitching post and swore. "Damn this town, damn them all to hell. Let the Ancestors take them." Wilcox saw Jimmy's pinched look and added. "You get, Jimmy. You take care of you and yours. There's not much time."

He watched as the young man ran down the long street.

It took him longer to get back to the Larkin ranch than he wanted. He was impatient to get moving on towards the mountains, to get back to Corwin. But the mare was not Corwin and couldn't keep up the pace he wanted.

He slowed the mare to a walk to let her rest some. He stood up in the stirrups and scanned the landscape. Small evergreens, a smattering of cacti, and big clumps of cheat grass covered the rolling landscape. He spotted hints of dust in the air between him and his destination.

"Damn," he mumbled, moving the mare towards the south. He

didn't know who or what was headed this way from the vicinity of the Larkin ranch, but he didn't want to run into them. "Damn," he said again as he spurred the mare into a trot.

***

HE SMELLED IT FIRST... OIL. WELL MAYBE NOT OIL, BUT something petroleum based, something that you almost never smelled on Valdrin away from the railroad. The rest of the worlds of the Alliance are filled with that smell--but not this one. It was just a tentative whiff, just a hint, but his olfactory senses, just like his hearing and eyesight, were the best that his money could buy when he was off world. He urged the mare into a gallop as the Larkin house came into view.

He breathed a sigh of relief when he spotted the cart and the horse. But his relief didn't last. The horse harnessed to the cart wasn't Corwin.

Sadie Larkin came striding out of the house carrying a large sack as Wilcox approached. "Where is he?" he asked.

"They came," she said with a set-jaw, determined look on her face as she swung the sack into the cart. "They seemed to know to come here. They took him." Her grim face met his as she added, "I'm sorry."

Wilcox slowly got off the tired mare and led her to the watering trough. He left her there to drink, walked several meters away, picked up a branch from the ground and started beating the fence with it. He didn't speak, he didn't make a sound, he just pounded the wrist-thick branch against the split rail fence until the branch broke. He then stood there panting, his face pinched in bitterness, holding the remaining piece of wood, looking around the Larkin ranch.

There was a small house with a tin roof. A lean-to and corral for the horses, now empty, an extensive garden, and the grave.

Except the grave looked different. Gone were the crude

wooden cross and the signs of freshly turned dirt. On top of it were some recently cut branches and straw.

Wilcox walked over, his eyes dangerous as he started clearing the grave with the branch he still held. Underneath the debris was fresh lye. The smell of it stung his nostrils as his efforts kicked it up into the air. He spit out the sour taste and turned and saw Sadie Larkin staring at him, her arms folded in front of her breasts.

"What is that you have to hide, Sadie Larkin?" he asked. "What the hell happened to my horse?"

"They came," she said, her eyes looking at the uncovered earth and not the man she was talking to. "They knew to come here. They knew to look here." Her eyes were wide, and Wilcox could smell the fear on her.

It helped diffuse his anger. "What is it you have to hide?" he repeated.

She nodded at the grave, her eyes filling with tears. "My husband, Jilop. He wasn't human. It's why we settled so far out of town."

"Not human?" Wilcox asked.

She tore her eyes away from the grave and looked at him. "Well, he looked human enough; he could pass if you didn't look too close or spend too much time with him. He was an anthropologist. He was here illegally, studying our 'technology constrained society.'"

Wilcox nodded. "And you were afraid they would find the body?"

She nodded looking back at the grave. "And his possessions."

Wilcox's eyes widened, but he didn't comment, he had other things on his mind. "And Corwin?"

"He saved me. There were only two of them. One had this device, a scanner I think, the other a gun. They would have found him... they would have found out..." She trailed off, her eyes going blank before she took a deep breath. Her face hardened and she squared her shoulders, walking back towards the house. Wilcox followed.

"Corwin spoke," she said looking back at him. "He saw what they were doing and he spoke. They would have found Jilop's body... they would have searched the house... they would have taken me away." She turned and looked at Wilcox. "Why did he do that?"

Wilcox shrugged and said, "He's a better man than I am."

Sadie wiped at her eyes and said, "Well, we must go. If they think about it too much, they'll be back to search." She marched towards the house and stopped when she got to the door and looked back. Wilcox hadn't followed. He stood still, his eyes vacant. "Are you going to help?" she asked.

He shook his head slowly. "I need your other horse, the stallion, the mare is spent."

"What?" she asked, walking back towards him.

"I can't leave Corwin to them, I can't. I'll either get him back or I'll put him down, but I will not let them have him."

"But..."

"Listen, I've got a place up in the mountains, up towards Helgold pass. An old mine I found while prospecting. You can go there. You'll be safe. It's hidden, hard to find, but I can draw you a map."

"Corwin... I'm sorry..." Sadie said, her hand coming to her mouth. "You'll never... they are too powerful."

"Can I take your other horse?" Wilcox asked, the muscles in his jaw bunching and releasing.

Sadie Larkin just stood there staring at him.

With a sigh, Wilcox asked, "How did you husband die?"

Her eyes went to the grave, and her mouth turned down. "He got sick, some damn virus foreign to him."

"Why didn't you take him to the doc in Salkin City? Our medical technology is less restricted--he might have been able to help."

Tears sprung to Sadie's eyes. "They would have exiled us, and I couldn't imagine leaving Valdrin. He said he would rather die than live without me."

Wilcox nodded sharply. "Then you understand why I have to go. Can I have the stallion?"

She shook her head as if waking from a dream, her eyes meeting Wilcox's again, "Yes, of course. But, please, just come with me. No good can come of this. You can't win."

"Yes, Ma'am, I know that. But for Corwin, I have to try."

WILCOX RODE THE STALLION HARD, NOT SAVING IT FOR A return trip. He was planning to ride Corwin out of Salkin City or not ride out at all.

The Ancestors weren't hard to find. They were in the center of town where the two main streets of Salkin City crossed, right out front of the Hitch Up Saloon.

He rode slowly down the road and studied them. They looked the same as he did--they were human--but he felt in awe of them. Men centuries old that had settled this planet, men his mother and father had taught him to revere. They had on what looked like glittering grey armor and held strange devices. Some looked like guns, others were small pieces of technology that fit in the palm of their hands that might do most anything.

There was a pile of contraband: flashlights, GPS units, cameras, batteries, solar chargers, mineral sniffers, and a few rock cutters. Wilcox wondered how they had done this so quickly. How they had found it all.

There were four of them gathered. Wilcox knew there were many more, but these four were making a display right in the center of town. A display, he knew, that was designed to chastise them all.

He let the stallion walk slowly towards them, and when he was fifty meters away, he slid off the horse and started walking towards the Ancestors.

"You don't steal a man's horse," he said loudly, his heart ponding in his ears.

"Do you speak, descendant?" One of them asked sharply. He was tall and thin with short black hair and a pinched look to his face. He rose up from the pile he was inspecting and turned towards Wilcox. The Ancestor pointed a device, some kind of sensor, at him and studied its readout. Wilcox could hear the faint whir of motors in the Ancestor's armor and smelled the stench of oil. He hated the hypocrisy of the Ancestors, using technology to enforce their ban on technology.

"You don't steal a man's horse," Wilcox said again. "We have laws against that around here." He swept back his duster so that his revolver was exposed. He didn't think a bullet could penetrate the Ancestor's armor, but his head was exposed, as well as gaps at the neck, waist, and joints. An Ancestor could die just like any man. It felt sacrilegious to even think it, but he had to for Corwin.

"And we have laws about the abuse of technology, laws that you seem to have no respect for."

Wilcox nodded. "I have no forbidden devices. Just me and my horse, the way God intended. Where is he? Where is Corwin?"

The man laughed and looked back down at the device in his palm, holding its display towards Wilcox. "No, you don't have any devices, just yourself. That is enough of an abomination."

Wilcox felt his anger overwhelming his awe and fear. He blinked once, then twice, his lips twitching into the briefest of smiles. During that span of blinks, he drew his gun, fired, and holstered it. When he was done, the device the Ancestor had held up was destroyed, and the Ancestor was holding his hand grimacing in pain.

"Where is Corwin?" he asked again. "I am just about done being polite."

The tall Ancestor shrugged and said, "There are many horses. How am I to know which one is yours?"

"He talks," Wilcox said. "He was taken from the Larkin Ranch east of here."

"Ah," the Ancestor said, "that thing. It's not too far."

Wilcox stiffened at hearing Corwin called a "thing," but he didn't comment, gesturing that the Ancestor should lead the way.

The armored man said to his fellows, "I'll take this descendant to his horse, you stay here." He then started walking down the street, his hands held awkwardly, well away from his body. Wilcox followed.

"Do you know why we forbid advanced technology on this planet?" The Ancestor asked. "Why we settled it this way? Why we enforce it so vigorously?"

"Valdrin is a preserve, created for a purer way of life, where man is not separate from nature or his creator, where man can live as God intended." Wilcox said, reciting the phrase all children learn.

The Ancestor looked over his shoulder and smiled at Wilcox. "Then you understand why we can't let a horse like Corwin, created as he was with advanced technology, be on this planet."

"I do not," Wilcox said. "His DNA is altered, sure, but he's pure biological. No 'advanced' technology in him. And he's sterile, so his DNA can't spread, can't ruin your precious balance. So, with all due respect, I think you got this one wrong."

The Ancestor stopped and turned. They were standing in front of the barbershop, and Wilcox could see multiple faces pressed to the windows. "Man is weak," the Ancestor said. "It makes me sad that I have to live the life I do." He flexed his armored arm. "That I have to live surrounded by technology, that I live only for a few months every generation to do this work. That I can't live the life we have afforded you. A life you don't seem to want." He sighed, his brown eyes looking through Wilcox as if at something far, far away. "I was born on the generational ship that brought us here. My ancestors taught me how this dry desert of a planet was all our movement was given, and we were lucky to have it. How we had to seed it with plants, animals, and a way of life from our past that was purer, simpler. That my generation had to guard it, had to keep coming back to make sure the intent was kept pure and not diluted by the passing generations."

His eyes snapped back into focus. "I know who you are, Wilcox," he said. "I know you struck it rich mining. I know you could have stayed, but you didn't. You turned your back on this life. If you wanted a life of technology, why didn't you stay away?"

Surprise registered on Wilcox's face as he struggled to understand how the Ancestors knew his story. "I was young and stupid when I left, a kid with way too much money. I learned a lot when I was gone. I missed my home, and what was done was done."

"And the horse?"

"One does not discard one's friends," Wilcox said, his voice low. He heard footsteps behind him and whirled around, his gun ready, but it was too late. One of the other Ancestors pointed a two-barreled contraption at him. It had a single grip, with two barrels about five inches apart. Wilcox felt an assault of sound slam into him, and his hands went involuntarily to his ears as he fell to his knees.

He knew what it was: a sonic gun. Non-lethal, the two barrels focused complementary sound waves on a single spot, silent to everyone but him. He thumbed the back of his left ear, turning his hearing down, but it wasn't enough. They knew him; they must have turned the thing all the way up. The sound crashed into him relentlessly. He couldn't think. He couldn't move. He screamed.

THE SMELL OF URINE ASSAULTED WILCOX AS HE SLOWLY WOKE up. His tongue felt swollen, his saliva thick, his mouth cottony. He felt a cot beneath him and could hear someone breathing nearby. He sat up slowly and held his head. It hurt like a railroad spike had been driven into it. As his eyes focused, he saw that he was locked in a cell, and Taylor was sitting outside it on a chair watching him. Wilcox's frown became a grimace.

"Good morning," Taylor said with a big smile.

"What do you want, Taylor?"

The big man shrugged. "To gloat. I'll admit it. I'm here to gloat. Your fancy mods, your horse, your wasted money, and you end up right where you belong." Taylor's chuckle was as irritating as fingernails on a chalkboard.

Wilcox took a slow deep breath and sighed. "Well, get it over with, Taylor." Wilcox raised his head and sniffed the air. "Is that you I smell?"

Taylor chuckled. "No, my friend, I believe you pissed yourself when they shot you with that gizmo. It's you that stinks."

Wilcox looked down and saw that Taylor was right. "At least I know right from wrong," Wilcox said.

Taylor chuckled again. "Sure. Going off planet and smuggling back your highly modded self and that abomination of a horse is the right thing to do. In the only place where humanity is still pure. Why don't you explain how that was the right thing to do?"

Wilcox stared at him and noticed the big man's new clothes, hat, boots, and pair of revolvers. He remembered Taylor buying drinks, getting half the town drunk right before the Ancestors came. Something sparked in his mind. "You didn't find any iridium. You're helping the Ancestors, and they're paying you, aren't they? You were buying drinks so no one would notice them coming."

Taylor stood and clapped, coming close to the bars of Wilcox's cell. "I guess it turns out you're not quite as stupid as you look."

"And that's how they knew where to go, how to take me down, about Corwin."

Taylor spat on the floor when Wilcox said "Corwin." "Thank God that abomination won't be alive much longer."

"What?" Wilcox asked, coming fully awake.

"You, they're going to exile. Him, they're going to make an example of."

Wilcox surged to his feet. Taylor saw the movement and shoved himself back, but he wasn't quick enough. Wilcox thrust his arm through the bars and got his hand around Taylor's throat.

"Hands where I can see them," Wilcox said. "Now you know so damn much about me, you know I can snap your neck long before you can draw."

Taylor nodded his head imperceptibly, his eyes wide.

"Where is Corwin?" Wilcox could feel Taylor's pulse against his hand thumping like a locomotive.

"He... he's behind the general store. They built an iron cage big enough for him."

"And what are they planning?"

"They are going to execute him at noon in front of the whole town." Wilcox's grip tightened and Taylor began to choke. "You kill... me... they hang you," he spit out.

Wilcox relaxed his grip but didn't let go. He looked around. His cell was in the little jail at the back of the Sheriff's office on the main strip. Sheriff Yost might have let Taylor back here to have his fun, but he wasn't dumb enough to give him a key. Wilcox jerked Taylor forward, his head bouncing off the iron bars of the cell, and he fell to the ground unconscious. Wilcox took the shiny new revolvers out of Taylor's holster and sat back on the cot and thought.

He needed to escape and quickly. But how? He could call for one of the deputies and force them to unlock him. And then what? Shoot his way out of the jail? He had no quarrel with Yost and his men.

As he sat there thinking he started to smell something. It was subtle at first, barely even noticeable, and then the alkaline stench of burning rock became apparent. He looked around and saw nothing but felt heat emanating from a corner of his cell.

Soon the rock cutter, the kind often used by miners to lay in dynamite charges, the kind the Ancestors were now confiscating, was visible as a red glow running along the rock forming a rough circle. Someone was breaking him out.

He searched Taylor, reaching through the bars of his cell, while the rock was cut. Wilcox took his money and put on his gun belt, holstering the revolvers.

When the red glow stopped, Wilcox moved the bed so it was up against the bars and sat on the floor of the cell, his back to the bed and pushed the rock with his feet. The wall was thick and the rock was heavy--it took everything he had, but he managed to slowly push it through.

"Hurry," a voice whispered through the open hole.

Wilcox squeezed through the opening and stood up in the alley behind the jail. There he saw Sadie Larkin, her black hair disheveled, the rock cutter at her feet. "We've got to go. Now. I've got the cart hid just outside town." She pointed south.

"Corwin?" Wilcox asked as he patted at his smoldering clothing, burned by the still hot rock

She shrugged her shoulders.

"I thank you for the escape, Ma'am, but I've got to go get Corwin. They're going to execute him. Head for the mountains. I'll catch up with you if I can."

She looked at him and frowned. "I won't be breaking you out of jail again. I felt bad about getting you mixed up in this and losing Corwin, but we're even now."

"I understand. But I can't leave Corwin to them." He headed further down the alley towards the general store.

Two guards, Wilcox knew them both, stood right in front of the cage holding Corwin. He had seen three ancestors around the corner within shouting distance. Wilcox studied Corwin from his prone position at the edge of the alley. The horse looked fine and calm. Wilcox was neither, his heart pounding loudly in his ears.

Five minutes passed and a plan, one that had any chance of succeeding, eluded him. He didn't want to just throw his life, or Corwin's away. He didn't want to kill people he knew and liked. He didn't want to land back in jail, only to be banished from his home.

Ten more minutes passed, and he heard the clock tower strike once. It was 11:30, and with Corwin's execution happening at noon, time was running out.

With a shrug, Wilcox pulled himself up, dusted himself off, pulled out Taylor's shiny new revolvers and stepped out of the alley.

The first guard, Adams, made to draw his gun. "I wouldn't do that, both you boys know how fast I am."

Adams bit his lip and put his hands out to the side.

The other guard, an apprentice mortician named Haut, did the same. He said, "You can't get away with the horse, Wilcox. Just turn back around, and we won't tell no one that you were here. Go hide, wait out the Ancestors. I hate to have to fit you for a coffin."

Wilcox nodded and stepped forward, a gun trained on each man. "That is some good advice, Haut. Sorry to say I can't take it. The Ancestors stole my horse and I can't let that stand."

Haut nodded his head, and Adams kept looking over his shoulder.

"You okay, Corwin?" Wilcox asked.

"Okay," Corwin replied. "Go now."

"That's the idea, my friend."

Just as Wilcox was wondering what Adams was waiting for, an Ancestor came around the corner. It was the same one he had talked to in front of the saloon. "Is it ready yet?" he asked. "We need to get it to..." He trailed off when he saw Wilcox, his face becoming more pinched than normal.

"Hands where I can see them," Wilcox said.

The Ancestor smiled and slowly raised his hands. "You don't want to do this," he said.

"Now you know my mind?" Wilcox asked. "Go over there and unlock the cage."

The Ancestor slowly walked to the cage. As he approached he said, "Getting the key, don't shoot." He reached into the pocked on the right leg of his armor and came out with an iron key. He unlocked the cage and stepped back, moving away from Adams and Haut.

"That's far enough," Wilcox said. "Now all three of you kindly stand together, over there." He indicated the other side of the alley with his gun. The three of them complied. "Now Corwin, just push the gate and you can walk out."

The big horse shook his head and stamped his front hooves. "Locked," he said.

"It's okay, boy. He unlocked it; you can just push your way out."

"Locked," the horse repeated with a snort.

Wilcox cursed under his breath. Smart, though Corwin was, he was also real dumb in some ways. All closed gates and doors were locked to him. "Don't follow me," Wilcox said as he backed over to the cage, his guns trained on the three men. "I will be much less kind if we meet again."

"You can't hide," the Ancestor said. "We will find you."

Wilcox hooked the cage with his boot cracking it open while watching the men. He stepped back, and now that the gate was cracked, Corwin pushed his way through. "Free," the horse said.

Wilcox holstered one revolver while keeping the other one trained on the three men as he mounted Corwin.

"Coming," Corwin said as Wilcox heard voices from around the corner. He pulled the second gun and began shooting. He shot over the heads of the three men and at the corner of the building he heard the voices coming from. The three threw themselves to the ground, covering their heads. He heard shouts from around the corner.

"Run, Corwin!"

WILCOX STAYED LOW ON THE BACK OF CORWIN AS BULLETS whizzed past them. He didn't urge his horse or even use the reins. Corwin knew what the stakes were so Wilcox stayed out of his way.

They had four mounted pursuers, three Ancestors and Taylor. When returning fire he always aimed at Taylor. Despite his recent history with them, he couldn't bring himself to shoot at the Ancestors. They were the Ancestors, beings of legend, centuries old, one did not shoot them. But Taylor was another story; Wilcox thought of him as a traitor. Eventually Taylor dropped back and it was just the three Ancestors chasing him.

They wound through the dusty streets of Salkin City at a gallop. Past the slaughterhouse, the cloying scent of blood clogging the air. Past the lumber mill, the scream of the saws assaulting their ears. Past the brothel where painted ladies waved and shouted as they went by.

Corwin was fast and soon his speed gained them distance from their pursuers, and they broke out of town with the Ancestors far behind.

Wilcox knew that Sadie Larkin and her wagon were headed south, so he headed north and west into the rough foothills of the mountain. He let Corwin slow his pace, keeping the Ancestors out of rifle range. This was now a marathon, not a sprint. There was a long way to go to reach safety.

THE ANCESTORS WERE ARMORED AND HEAVIER ON THEIR mounts than Wilcox. Soon the gap between them grew enough so that Wilcox was comfortable giving Corwin a break.

He let the horse drink his fill at a small creek and then walked with him up a mountain trail for a while.

"Ancestors gone?" Corwin asked as he followed Wilcox.

"No, Corwin. Not really. They are still chasing us."

"Where go?" the horse asked.

"I'm not sure. The plan was to hole up in that old mine. But with them on our trail I don't want to lead them to it." Wilcox stopped when he realized that Corwin wasn't following anymore. The horse was still, his nostrils wide. Wilcox thumbed the back of his ear and listened. He heard the creek they had left behind as it made its way to the low lands. He heard the wind whistling through the pinon trees. He heard a grunt and the click of a rifle hammer being pulled back.

"Run!" Wilcox yelled as he leaped for cover. A sting and then a sensation of fire burst forth from his shoulder before he heard the shot. His dive turned into an awkward roll as he heard the sound of Corwin's hooves thundering up the trail.

He looked at his shoulder. It was bleeding but looked to be only a flesh wound. He crawled behind a rock and listened again. More shots and the sound of Corwin's receding hooves. The pattern of his run didn't change, so Wilcox guessed they didn't get him. That was something.

He wondered how they had caught up with him. The three pursuing Ancestors were far behind. Radio, it had to be radio. While the Ancestors didn't allow modern technology on this planet, they were using it in the pursuit of their goal. The irony of it was bitter in Wilcox's mouth.

He listened carefully and heard some whispers and men moving in the forest above him. He counted four different sets of footsteps moving in to flank him on either side.

"Hold on, boys," he shouted. "Let's talk this over before people start dying."

"Surrender and no one has to die," a voice said back. It was deep and gravely like stone against stone. It wasn't a young voice; it was a voice hard with the lessons of age.

"Let me go and no one has to die," Wilcox said.

"I can't do that," the gravel voice replied.

"And you've got me backed into a corner. I won't go down without a fight." Wilcox paused as he checked his revolvers. Six bullets in both of them, twelve more bullets in the belt. Not enough. "I was taught to revere the Ancestors. Please don't test me. I don't want to kill you."

The man with the gravel voice chuckled and said, "Hold it there, boys. Take cover and watch his position." Wilcox could hear that the movement stopped. "Wilcox, I am laying my gun down and coming to your location. I want to talk, are you willing?"

"Willing, I am. One hostile move, though, and I will kill you."

"Understood. Here I come."

Wilcox listened to a single set of footsteps approach him. "Hands up, if you don't mind," Wilcox said, pointing one of his revolvers at the Ancestor. He was tall, over two meters, but wasn't wearing armor like the other Ancestors. He wore buckskins and looked at home in the forest. He had a weathered face and short grey hair. The only thing that betrayed him as an Ancestor was the radio perched on his right ear.

His hands remained in the air as he walked below Wilcox and turned around.

"See, unarmed," he said.

Wilcox pointed at the large knife strapped to his leg. "You call that unarmed?"

The Ancestor smiled again, betraying his origins. His teeth were straight, white and perfect. The perfection of them was disconcerting in his weathered face. "Oh come now, we both know how fast you are."

"Say your piece," Wilcox said.

The Ancestor squatted down, his grey eyes boring into Wilcox.

"You can't escape. If you give yourself up, we won't hurt you, but you will have to leave the planet."

"Sorry, done that. Not doing it again."

"Why waste your life like this?"

Wilcox's shrug turned into a grimace as the pain in his shoulder intensified. "When I went off world, I thought it would be this grand adventure. And it was, but soon it soured on me like fresh milk in the noon-day sun. It wasn't for me. This is my home, I ain't leaving."

A brief smile danced on the older man's face before he reached into his vest. Wilcox cocked his gun and the older man withdrew his hand. "My name's Blane," he said. "And I was just going for a flask, if you don't mind. I figure we ought to have a drink before the dying starts."

Wilcox nodded but kept his gun steady on him as Blane withdrew a metal flask, unscrewed the top and took a sip, a sigh escaping his lips. He handed the flask to Wilcox. He sniffed it and took a sip, the liquid burning his throat as he suppressed a cough. "Strong stuff," he said. This wasn't any fancy whisky Blane had given him, but plain old corn mash gin. The kind of drink a man makes for himself from corn he grew himself.

Blane nodded, "If it ain't gonna kick you in the head, why drink it?"

"Are you really an Ancestor?" Wilcox asked, taking another sip and handing the flask back.

Blane chuckled and nodded. "I reckon I am at this point. I've been through two long sleeps, so that does qualify me as an Ancestor."

His eyes wide, Wilcox looked Blane over again. He wasn't an original Ancestor. Wilcox had never heard of them recruiting. But, it didn't matter now; he had bought Corwin enough time to get away. "Well, we've had our drink. Shall we start this dance?"

"I reckon," Blane said as he put the flask away and rose. "Okay, boys," he said loudly. "Hold your positions until I am back to where

I put down my gun. And then..." he trailed off not finishing the thought.

"Thanks for the drink," Wilcox said as the older man walked away. "I'll be sorry to kill you."

———

THE ROCK WILCOX HID BEHIND WAS HIS SHIELD AND HIS downfall. It offered protection, but it didn't give him an avenue to strike back without exposing himself. He tried, multiple times, but there were two riflemen keeping him pinned down. Each time he showed his head it nearly got shot off. The other two were moving into flanking positions and it wouldn't be long.

He looked at the rough terrain that sloped down below him to the creek. There were a few pine trees, but it was mostly smaller pinon still. Not much good cover. And if he did get away, what then? Was he going to outrun four horsed men? Ones that could call in reinforcements from a different direction. Ones that could watch him from satellites.

Wilcox grunted and refilled his revolvers with the last of his bullets and prepared to continue the fight. He had gotten a bead on one of the riflemen keeping him pinned down, and it was time to make them pay the price. If he was going to die, he wasn't going to do it alone.

He took his hat off and held it with his left hand while holding one of the revolvers in his right. Still hunkered behind the rock, he raised his hat and was rewarded with gunfire from both riflemen. They were a bit overzealous, and he knew they would both need to reload soon. When the fire abated, he rose up enough and fired at the one of the riflemen. His effort was met with a cry of pain, but he had been too soon. The other rifleman had been bluffing, another shot rang out, and Wilcox went down.

———

WILCOX FELT THE WARM, VELVET NOSE OF CORWIN IN HIS hands. "Hold on, boy, I'll get more," Wilcox said, reaching into the bag of oats and taking out a huge handful and holding it for him. The horse ate eagerly, gently scooping the grain into his mouth with his soft lips and chewing them with his large teeth.

Wilcox laughed as the horse pushed his head against Wilcox's chest, asking for more. "Still hungry, huh?" he asked, but the horse didn't answer. The man thought it strange but was so happy to be with his friend that he didn't think anything of it.

As he reached into the bag of oats again, he felt his scalp burning, a line of bright pain on the right side of his head where he parted his brown hair. He felt the warm trickle of blood and the pain wax and wane with each heartbeat.

Nausea flooded him, and he felt the hard ground underneath him and smelled gunpowder and blood. Dreaming, he had been dreaming.

"He's down," a voice shouted. "Looks like I got him in the head. Is Lindstrom Okay? The freak just winged him right?"

Wilcox heard the cautious steps of the Ancestor that had shouted. The one that had shot him. The one that would kill him if he realized he wasn't dead. He felt the smooth grip of a revolver in his hand and was glad.

Adrenaline flowed through his veins, and ignoring the pain in his head and in his shoulder he sat up quickly cocking the revolver and pointing it at the Ancestor.

A wave of dizziness assaulted him and he wanted to throw up, but he pushed the sensations down and focused on his target who was turning back towards him. "One move," Wilcox hissed, "and you die."

The Ancestor had blond hair and a beard and wore the segmented armor of the Ancestors. He looked at Wilcox, eyes wide, and started to pull his rifle up.

"Was I not clear?" Wilcox asked, and the Ancestor lowered his rifle. "Slowly set the gun down. Keep your hands where I can see them." The Ancestor complied. "Now back up a pace." Wilcox moved slowly, he didn't want his enemy to see how dizzy he was, and took the rifle.

"Well?" Blane shouted as he walked down towards Wilcox and the other Ancestor, "Is he dead?"

"Not quite," Wilcox said as Blane came into view. He had drawn his second revolver and had one pointed at each of the men.

Blane smiled and held his hands out to the side, one of those hands held a rifle. "Good," he said, his gravel voice loud. "I would rather you not die. You seem a decent sort to me."

"Toss your rifle this way, easy," Wilcox demanded. The older man complied. Wilcox scooted the rifle towards him with his foot. "Now the revolver, I..." Another wave of nausea hit Wilcox as his vision blurred. In that brief second, Blane's hand reached his revolver and had it half pulled. "Oh, no you don't. Two fingers, easy, toss it to me."

Blane complied, a sour look on his grizzled face. "You should just kill us and get it over with," he said loudly.

"I thought I was a 'decent sort,'" Wilcox replied, licking his lips. He knew he was right; there were two more Ancestors out there and both of them armed. "Go stand next to your buddy there."

Wilcox watched as Blane slowly moved to stand next to the blond-haired Ancestor. He moved slightly so the two men were between him and the rifleman he had shot.

"Now," Wilcox shouted, realizing that Blane had signaled to the other two Ancestors that he was alive when he spoke loudly, "If I hear one branch break, one footstep come towards us, I will kill these men. Got that?"

"Understood," someone yelled from the where the rifleman was.

"What now?" Blane asked. "Two more armed men out there, reinforcements on the way. We've got radio and satellites. What do you expect is going to happen here, Wilcox?"

"I expect that I'm going to get away. The choice you need to make is if I will leave with you alive or dead."

"Well, I would prefer alive, if you don't mind."

"Very well then. Both of you turn your backs to me and call your other two boys over. Have them approach with their hands up holding their guns well away from their bodies."

Blane sighed and turned around, as did the other Ancestor. "Did you hear that boys?" he yelled.

"Yes, sir," a voice said from the trees.

"So you all do as he said. That's an order."

Wilcox gritted his teeth against another wave of nausea. He was glad Blane couldn't see him. The bleeding had slowed, and the trickle of it dripping down his face was an aggravating tickle he was desperate to deal with, but he needed both hands.

The third and fourth Ancestors walked over, one supporting the other. The one had his hand pressed to his neck, blood running freely.

"Stand with your comrades and toss your weapons onto the pile," Wilcox said. After they had complied he added, "Now turn around, hands up."

Wilcox considered killing them. They had tried to kill him, they would keep following him. But he couldn't do it. He couldn't shoot a man in the back, much less four Ancestors. He holstered one gun and began pulling the lacing out of one of his buckskin boots. He squatted down and used the lace to roughly bind the rifles and pistols together, so he could carry them with one hand.

"Where are the horses?" he asked.

"They are tied up the hill a bit," Blane answered his upraised hand pointing.

"Now this is how it's going to go, gentlemen." I am going to move away and ride out of here. As I leave I will keep my eye on you. If you all move one muscle I will shoot to kill. Understood?"

"Understood," Blane said.

Wilcox paused, rubbing the blood off his face with his sleeve. It was beginning to drip over his right eye. As he bent to pick up the guns he had bound together, he groaned, another wave of nausea hitting him.

Out of the corner of his eye, Wilcox saw the blur of movement and instinct took over. He dropped all the way to the ground and fired at his prisoners. A knife whistled over his head, a man fell, the other men ran. Wilcox continued to fire from his prone position at the receding Ancestors until his gun emptied.

The smell of gun smoke and blood assaulted him and he vomited, unable to hold down the nausea any longer. He slowly rose, his remaining loaded gun in hand, his shoulder sore and his head throbbing. He saw one body on the ground. Blane. He could hear the other three Ancestors as they ran through the forest away from him, the one with the neck wound moving slowly and still visible.

He ignored them and approached the fallen Ancestor. Blane had thrown the knife. Blane had not been armored. He lay flat on his back, his eyes blinking slowly, blood seeping out of his chest soaking the ground beneath him.

Wilcox squatted down, Blane's wide eyes meeting him. "Why?" Wilcox asked.

The man gasped for breath, but did not speak, his mouth moving like a fish out of water. It didn't last long. Soon the gasping ended and the eyes, now vacant, stared up at the sky.

Wilcox swore loudly before gently closing the dead man's eyes. "I'm sorry," he whispered, nausea rolling over him again. But this time he couldn't tell if it was from the head wound or the aftermath of killing a man. Killing an Ancestor.

He slowly rose, holstered his guns, and gathered the guns he had taken from the Ancestors. He made his slow way up the hill to where the Ancestors had left their horses.

"Hurt," Corwin said as he nuzzled Wilcox with his soft

nose. The horse had found him shortly after he had gotten clear of the ambush site with the Ancestor's four horses.

"Yeah," Wilcox said, his head aching. "We need to move, though. They are going to be after us."

"Why?"

"Because we're different Corwin. You are different than other horses, and I am different than other men."

"Good."

Wilcox chuckled as he tied the rope that he had been leading the four horses with to Wilcox's saddle. He mounted Corwin and said, "Take us up, boy, up over the mountains."

Corwin snorted, turned back to the four horses and whinnied, like he was telling them something, and then surged forth.

THE CAMPFIRE BURNED LOW IN THE COOL NIGHT. WILCOX squatted on the ground studying it. A lone figure sat at attention next to it. He smelled rabbit stew and heard the crackle of the fire. He studied the profile of the figure until he was as sure as he could be.

He walked slowly into the fire light, holding his hands away from his body. The woman by the fire leveled a double-barreled shotgun at him and said, "That's far enough. I don't want trouble."

"Seems to me," Wilcox said, "that a woman alone all the way out here with the Ancestors on the loose, purging Valdrin of illegal tech, has already found trouble."

"Wilcox?"

"Yes, Mrs. Larkin, it's me."

"I thought..." she began as she studied him in the dim firelight. "You're hurt." She threw another log on the fire, new flames illuminating Wilcox's face. "Get over here, now, and let me tend to you."

"Yes, Ma'am." Wilcox said as he brushed at the ugly scab on his scalp. He hadn't given it the tending it needed.

"Corwin?" she asked, her voice a whisper.

"He's fine," he said. "I left him back a ways, just in case."

She dabbed at his wound with a cloth and Wilcox winced. "What happened?"

Wilcox told her, or rather he summarized briefly the chase of the Ancestors and how he got away.

"Did they follow?"

He shook his head. "We went over the mountains into the Great Waste. I nearly killed Corwin and myself doing it. It was more than a normal horse could have done. If they followed, they died, and I don't think their satellites could find us once we got back into the forest."

"And now?"

"And now we go into hiding. It occurred to me that I never got around to drawing that map, so I came back to find you. I have that old mine setup and ready. It won't be much of a life, but it will be a life."

Sadie Larkin looked into Wilcox's eyes and slowly nodded.

EVAN WILCOX SAT BACK IN THE MOUTH OF THE DAMP CAVE, hidden in the shadows. He could see the land rolling away from his high perch, but even the Ancestors wouldn't be able to see him where he was. He was alive and safe, but he missed being in the open, he missed riding Corwin.

It wasn't too bad. He had Corwin and Sadie Larkin for company. He had food and snuck out at night to go hunting. It wasn't much of a life, but...

He inhaled slowly and sighed. While his physical wounds were healing, he still hurt. He kept seeing Blane's fluttering eyes as the man breathed his last breath, as the Ancestor died.

He heard the sound of hooves on the ground behind him, but he didn't turn. He could smell a mixture of dirt and straw and horse flesh. He loved the smell of Corwin, almost more than the look of him. He breathed it in and felt himself calm.

"Think too much," the horse said, as he knocked Wilcox's hat off.

Wilcox laughed as Corwin's lips tugged at his hair as if he were going to eat it.

"Alive good," Corwin added.

"Yes it is, my friend. Yes it is."

AUTHOR'S NOTE

If you are not familiar with my work, I write a lot of different kinds of stories, different lengths, across different genres. Some of them a mashup like this one (western/sci-fi), I also have a series of first-person ghost stories, a zombie/adventure/romance serial (see, I really do like to mash genres together) and a superhero/love story series. As well as a wide array of genres in the shorter lengths.

I invite you to join my email newsletter. When you subscribe you get some free ebooks. We've got a program going on called Campfire Tales where my readers fill out a survey and I write a story with their input. And then, down the line a bit, they get to read it for free.

If you join now the last two Campfire Tale stories will be yours right away and there's usually a bonus story.

All it takes is an email and you can opt out at any time. Head over to RobertJMcCarter.com/CampfireTales

Thanks for reading. You can find me on facebook at: facebook.com/RobertJMcCarterAuthor or on twitter at: twitter.com/RobertJMcCarter

AFTERWORD

A FEW YEARS BACK, WHEN I WAS TRYING TO BECOME comfortable with the blank page, I spent morning after morning writing openings. I did this for months. I would start with nothing, no ideas, a blank screen, early in the morning before food or caffeine.

I wrote opening after opening after opening, until the blank page didn't scare me anymore. It does intimidate, I don't expect that to go away, but I don't fear it like I used to.

While I was doing that, some openings wouldn't leave me alone. The opening to this story is one of them. It was so curious. Who are these ancestors? How can a society that can engineer a talking horse be like a western? It wouldn't leave me alone.

I had a horse as kid, living on a ranch outside of Globe, Arizona. I rode him nearly daily for years through the cactus filled, high desert foothills of the Pinal Mountains, herding our milk cows back to the ranch. In some ways westerns are a bit of a natural fit for me, but I hadn't written anything in that genre.

I hadn't ridden in many years, but right before I wrote this opening, a good friend of mine let me take a ride on her horse. It felt... well, it felt good, and natural, and I remembered how much I had loved my horse and loved parts of that ranch life.

Horses are a tremendous commitment in time, money, and energy. If you look at our modern culture and see how we tend to get attached to our cars and our pets, now imagine combining those two. How attached would you become to a strong, intelligent animal that you depend on for survival?

That ride turned into this opening that wouldn't leave me alone and out popped this gritty sci-fi/western about the bond between a man and a talking horse.

This story received an honorable mention in the Writers of the Future Contest.

ABOUT THE AUTHOR

Robert J. McCarter is the author of six novels, three novellas, and dozens of short stories. He is a finalist for the *Writers of the Future* contest and his stories have appeared in *The Saturday Evening Post, Adomeda Spaceways Inflight Magazine, Everyday Fiction,* and numerous anthologies.

He has written a series of first person ghost novels (starting with Shuffled Off: A Ghost's Memoir) and a superhero / love story series (Neutrinoman and Lightningirl, A Love Story), as well as two short story collections.

Of his latest novel, *Seeing Forever,* Kirkus Reviews says, "Sci-fi as it should be: engaging, moving, and grand in scope."

Find out more at:
robertjmccarter.com

BOOKS BY ROBERT J. MCCARTER

Woody and June Versus the Apocalypse

1. Woody and June versus the Wannabe Warlord
2. Woody and June versus the Fungus-Head Zombies
3. Woody and June versus the Grand Canyon
4. Woody and June versus the Ex
5. Woody and June versus the Third Wheel
6. Woody and June versus Phantom Company (*coming August, 2019*)
7. Woody and June versus the Daring Rescue (*coming September, 2019*)

Join the Woody and June Fan Club at WoodyAndJune.com

Novels in the "Ghost's Memoir" world:

- Shuffled Off: A Ghost's Memoir, Book 1
- Drawing the Dead
- To Be a Fool: A Ghost's Memoir, Book 2
- Of Things Not Seen: A Ghost's Memoir, Book 3

Other Novels:

- Seeing Forever

Books in the Neutrinoman and Lightningirl Series:

- Meteor Attack! Neutrinoman and Lightningirl, A Love Story. Episode 1
- Toxic Asset: Neutrinoman and Lightningirl, A Love Story. Episode 2
- Protocol X: Neutrinoman and Lightningirl, A Love Story. Episode 3
- Season 1 (Omnibus edition of Episodes 1 - 3)
- Off Book: Neutrinoman and Lightningirl, A Love Story. Episode 4 (*Coming soon*)

Walter Anchor, Ghost Detective Stories

- **Case 1: "Detecting Haley"** (also part of *Life After: Stories of Life, Death, and the Places in Between*)
- **Case 2: "The Ghost Brides Gift"** (exclusive to newsletter subscribers)
- **Case 3: "A Long Hard Fall"** (coming in 2019)

For a complete list of Walter Anchor stories, go to RobertJMcCarter.com/WalterAnchor

Short Stores and Collections

- Life After: Stories of Life, Death, and the Places in Between
- Anomalous Readings: Thirteen Curious and Confounding Tales
- Probability: Resolve
- The Turing Test Will Be Televised

- Ghost Hacker, Zombie Maker

  For a complete list, go to RobertJMcCarter.com